MY LITTLE PONY

FRIENDS FOREVER

RAINBOW DASH & SPITFIRE

Written by
Ted Anderson

Art by
Jay Fosgitt

Colors by
Heather Breckel

Lettered by
Neil Uyetake

 Spotlight

ABDOPUBLISHING.COM

Reinforced library bound edition published in 2019 by Spotlight, a division of ABDO, PO Box 398166, Minneapolis, Minnesota 55439. Spotlight produces high-quality reinforced library bound editions for schools and libraries. Published by agreement with IDW.

Printed in the United States of America, North Mankato, Minnesota.
042018
092018

THIS BOOK CONTAINS RECYCLED MATERIALS

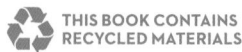

Licensed By:

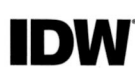

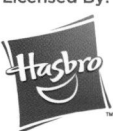

Library of Congress Control Number: 2017961346

Publisher's Cataloging in Publication Data

Names: Anderson, Ted, author. | Fosgitt, Jay; Breckel, Heather; Uyetake, Neil, illustrators.
Title: Rainbow Dash & Spitfire / by Ted Anderson; illustrated by Jay Fosgitt, Heather Breckel and Neil Uyetake.
Description: Minneapolis, MN : Spotlight, 2019 | Series: My little pony: friends forever set 2
Summary: Spitfire asks for Rainbow Dash's help to train the Junior Flyers Summer Camp.
Identifiers: ISBN 9781532142406 (lib. bdg.)
Subjects: LCSH: My Little Pony (Trademark)--Juvenile fiction. | Camps--Management--Juvenile fiction. | Flying--Juvenile fiction. | Helpfulness--Juvenile fiction. | Comic books, strips, etc.--Juvenile fiction.
Classification: DDC 741.5--dc23

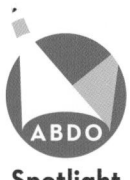

Spotlight

A Division of ABDO
abdopublishing.com

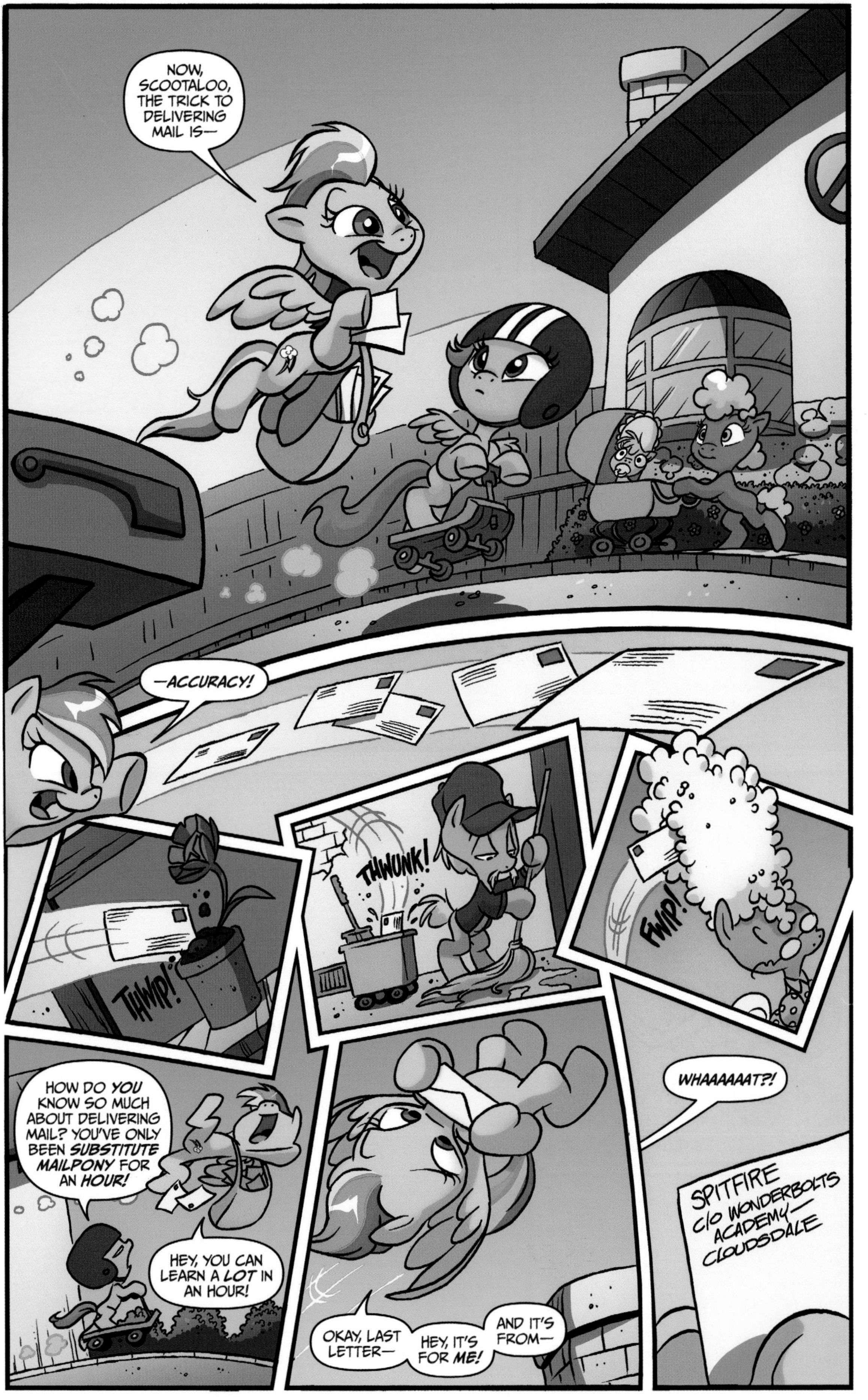
NOW, SCOOTALOO, THE TRICK TO DELIVERING MAIL IS—
—ACCURACY!
THWIP!
THWUNK!
FWIP!
HOW DO *YOU* KNOW SO MUCH ABOUT DELIVERING MAIL? YOU'VE ONLY BEEN *SUBSTITUTE MAILPONY* FOR AN *HOUR!*
HEY, YOU CAN LEARN A *LOT* IN AN HOUR!
OKAY, LAST LETTER—
HEY, IT'S FOR *ME!*
AND IT'S FROM—
WHAAAAAAT?!
SPITFIRE
C/O WONDERBOLTS ACADEMY—
CLOUDSDALE

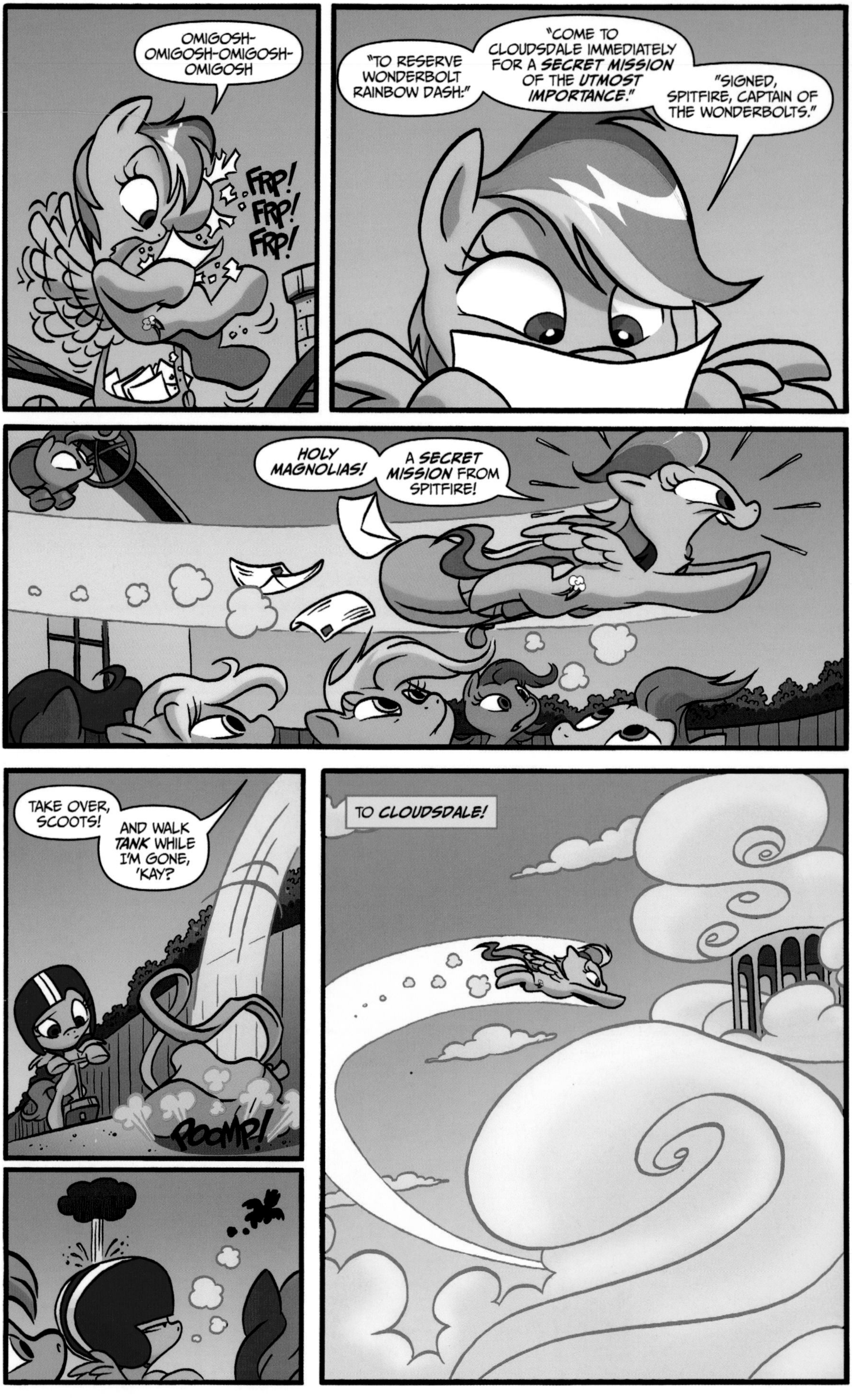
OMIGOSH-OMIGOSH-OMIGOSH-OMIGOSH
FRP! FRP! FRP!
"TO RESERVE WONDERBOLT RAINBOW DASH:"
"COME TO CLOUDSDALE IMMEDIATELY FOR A SECRET MISSION OF THE UTMOST IMPORTANCE."
"SIGNED, SPITFIRE, CAPTAIN OF THE WONDERBOLTS."
HOLY MAGNOLIAS!
A SECRET MISSION FROM SPITFIRE!
TAKE OVER, SCOOTS!
AND WALK TANK WHILE I'M GONE, 'KAY?
POOMP!
TO CLOUDSDALE!

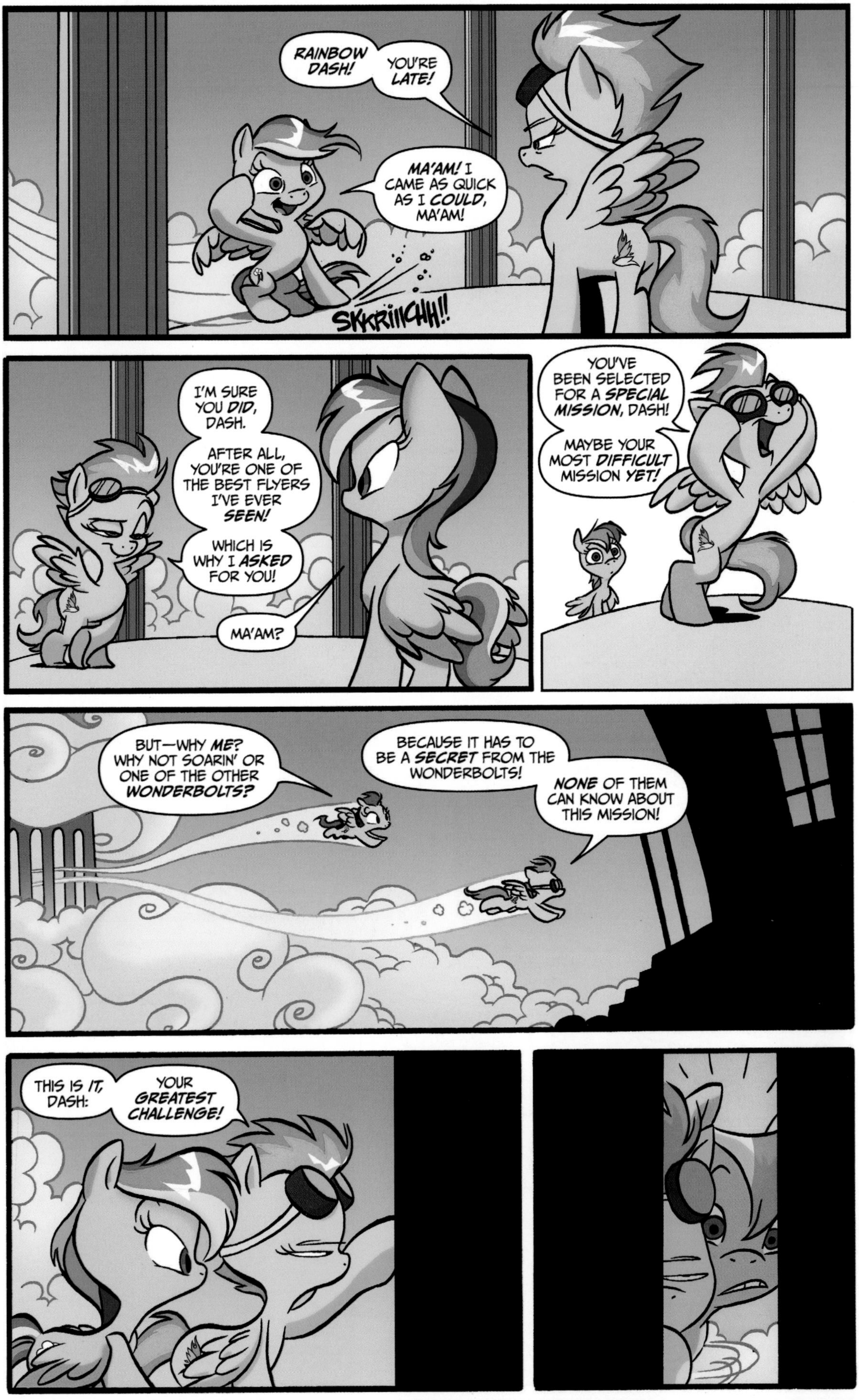

RAINBOW DASH!
YOU'RE LATE!
MA'AM! I CAME AS QUICK AS I COULD, MA'AM!
SKKRIIICHH!!
I'M SURE YOU DID, DASH.
AFTER ALL, YOU'RE ONE OF THE BEST FLYERS I'VE EVER SEEN!
WHICH IS WHY I ASKED FOR YOU!
MA'AM?
YOU'VE BEEN SELECTED FOR A SPECIAL MISSION, DASH!
MAYBE YOUR MOST DIFFICULT MISSION YET!
BUT—WHY ME? WHY NOT SOARIN' OR ONE OF THE OTHER WONDERBOLTS?
BECAUSE IT HAS TO BE A SECRET FROM THE WONDERBOLTS!
NONE OF THEM CAN KNOW ABOUT THIS MISSION!
THIS IS IT, DASH:
YOUR GREATEST CHALLENGE!

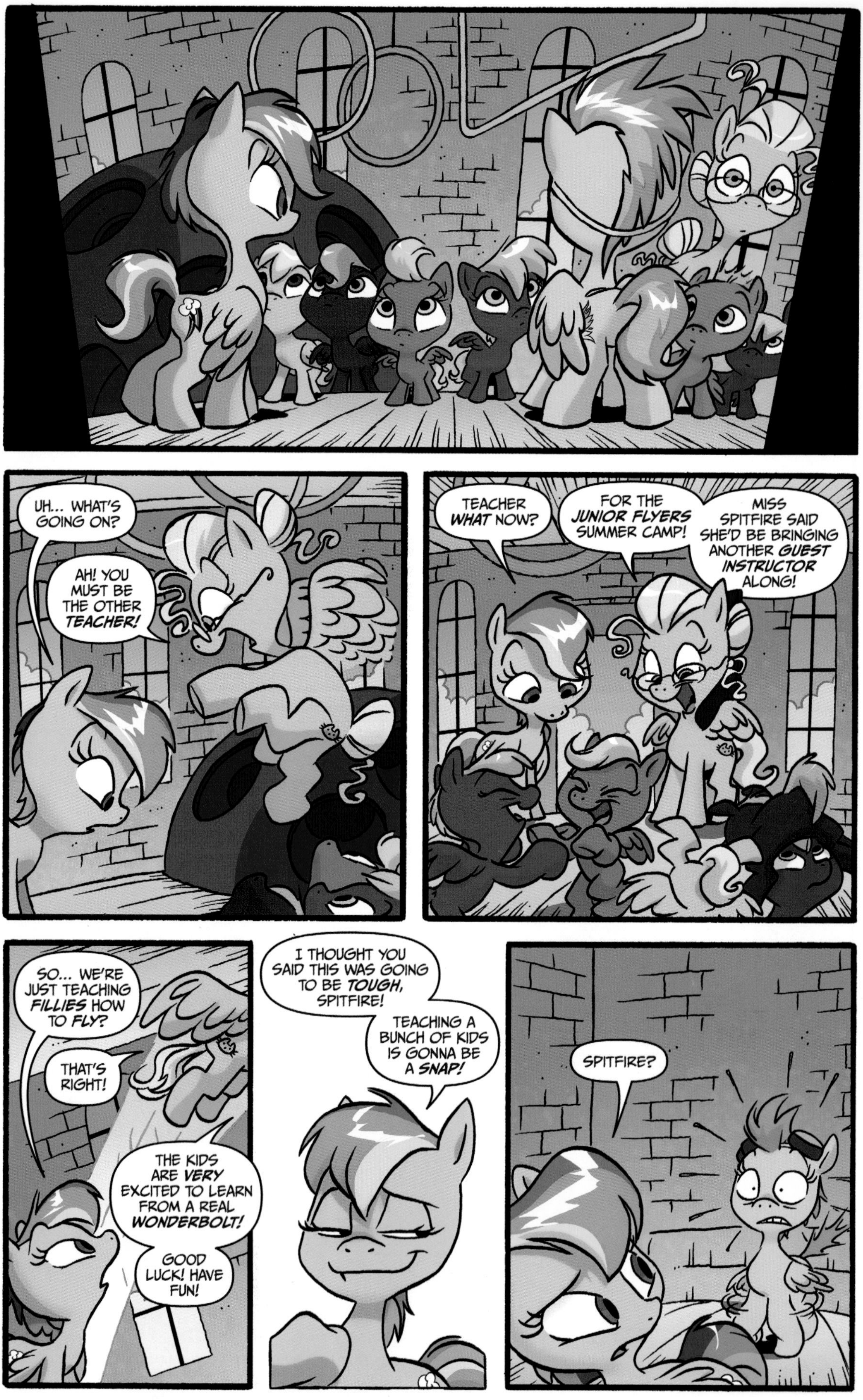

UH... WHAT'S GOING ON?
AH! YOU MUST BE THE OTHER TEACHER!
TEACHER WHAT NOW?
FOR THE JUNIOR FLYERS SUMMER CAMP!
MISS SPITFIRE SAID SHE'D BE BRINGING ANOTHER GUEST INSTRUCTOR ALONG!
SO... WE'RE JUST TEACHING FILLIES HOW TO FLY?
THAT'S RIGHT!
THE KIDS ARE VERY EXCITED TO LEARN FROM A REAL WONDERBOLT!
GOOD LUCK! HAVE FUN!
I THOUGHT YOU SAID THIS WAS GOING TO BE TOUGH, SPITFIRE!
TEACHING A BUNCH OF KIDS IS GONNA BE A SNAP!
SPITFIRE?

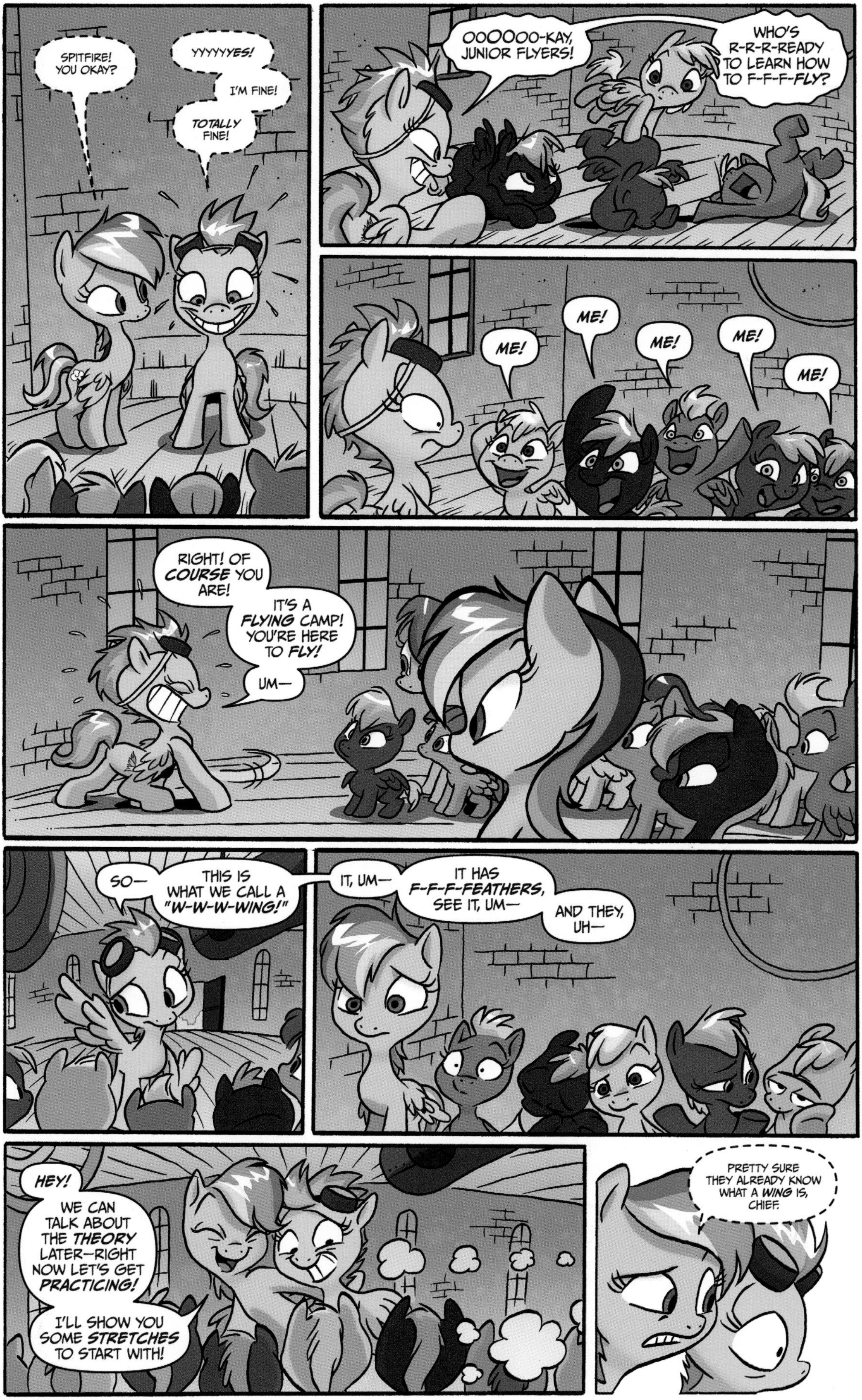
SPITFIRE! YOU OKAY?
YYYYYYES!
I'M FINE!
TOTALLY FINE!
OOOOOO-KAY, JUNIOR FLYERS!
WHO'S R-R-R-READY TO LEARN HOW TO F-F-F-FLY?
ME!
ME!
ME!
ME!
ME!
RIGHT! OF COURSE YOU ARE!
IT'S A FLYING CAMP! YOU'RE HERE TO FLY!
UM—
SO—
THIS IS WHAT WE CALL A "W-W-W-WING!"
IT, UM—
IT HAS F-F-F-FEATHERS, SEE IT, UM—
AND THEY, UH—
HEY!
WE CAN TALK ABOUT THE THEORY LATER—RIGHT NOW LET'S GET PRACTICING!
I'LL SHOW YOU SOME STRETCHES TO START WITH!
PRETTY SURE THEY ALREADY KNOW WHAT A WING IS, CHIEF.

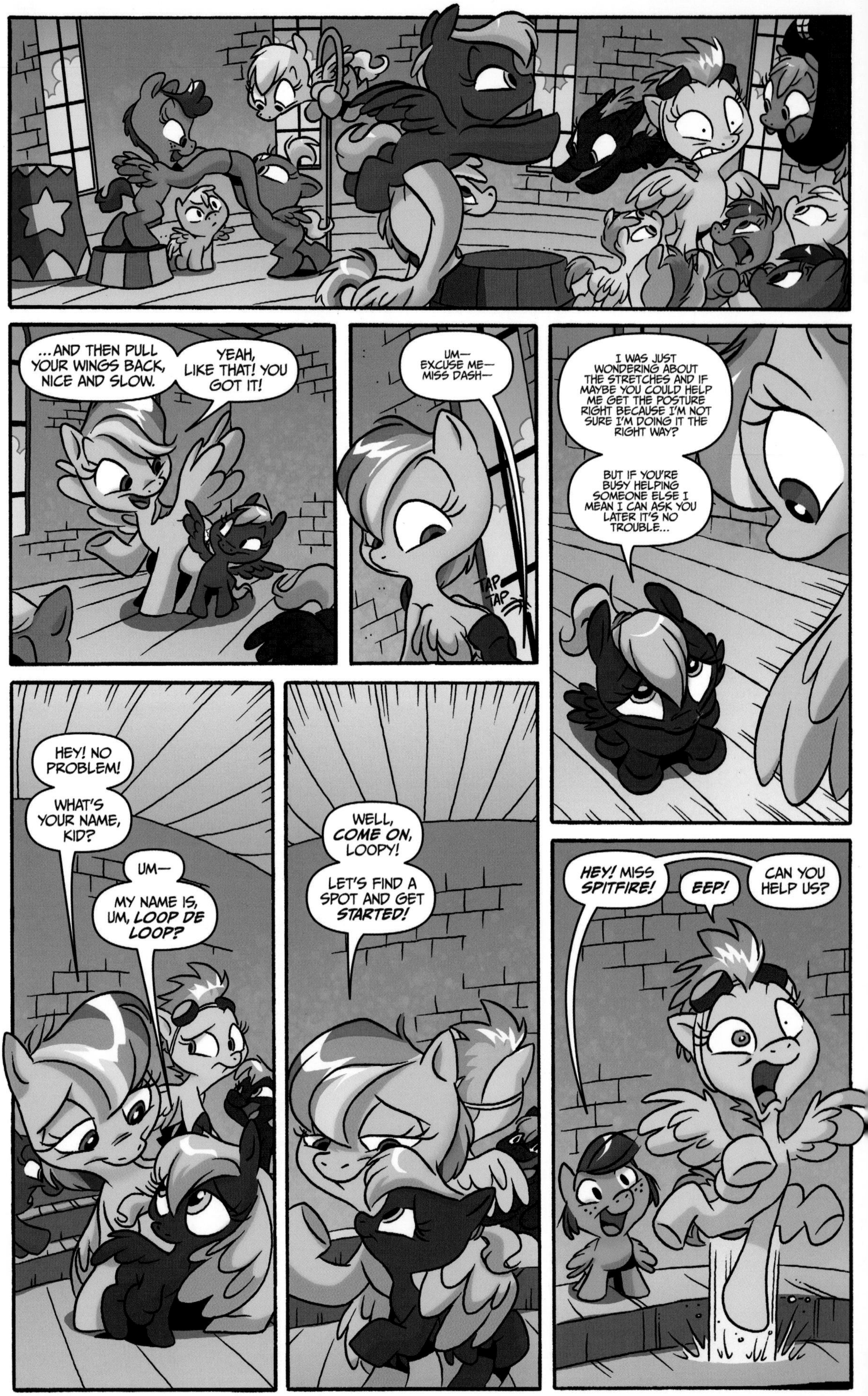
...AND THEN PULL YOUR WINGS BACK, NICE AND SLOW.
YEAH, LIKE THAT! YOU GOT IT!
UM— EXCUSE ME— MISS DASH—
TAP TAP
I WAS JUST WONDERING ABOUT THE STRETCHES AND IF MAYBE YOU COULD HELP ME GET THE POSTURE RIGHT BECAUSE I'M NOT SURE I'M DOING IT THE RIGHT WAY?
BUT IF YOU'RE BUSY HELPING SOMEONE ELSE I MEAN I CAN ASK YOU LATER IT'S NO TROUBLE...
HEY! NO PROBLEM!
WHAT'S YOUR NAME, KID?
UM—
MY NAME IS, UM, LOOP DE LOOP?
WELL, COME ON, LOOPY!
LET'S FIND A SPOT AND GET STARTED!
HEY! MISS SPITFIRE!
EEP!
CAN YOU HELP US?

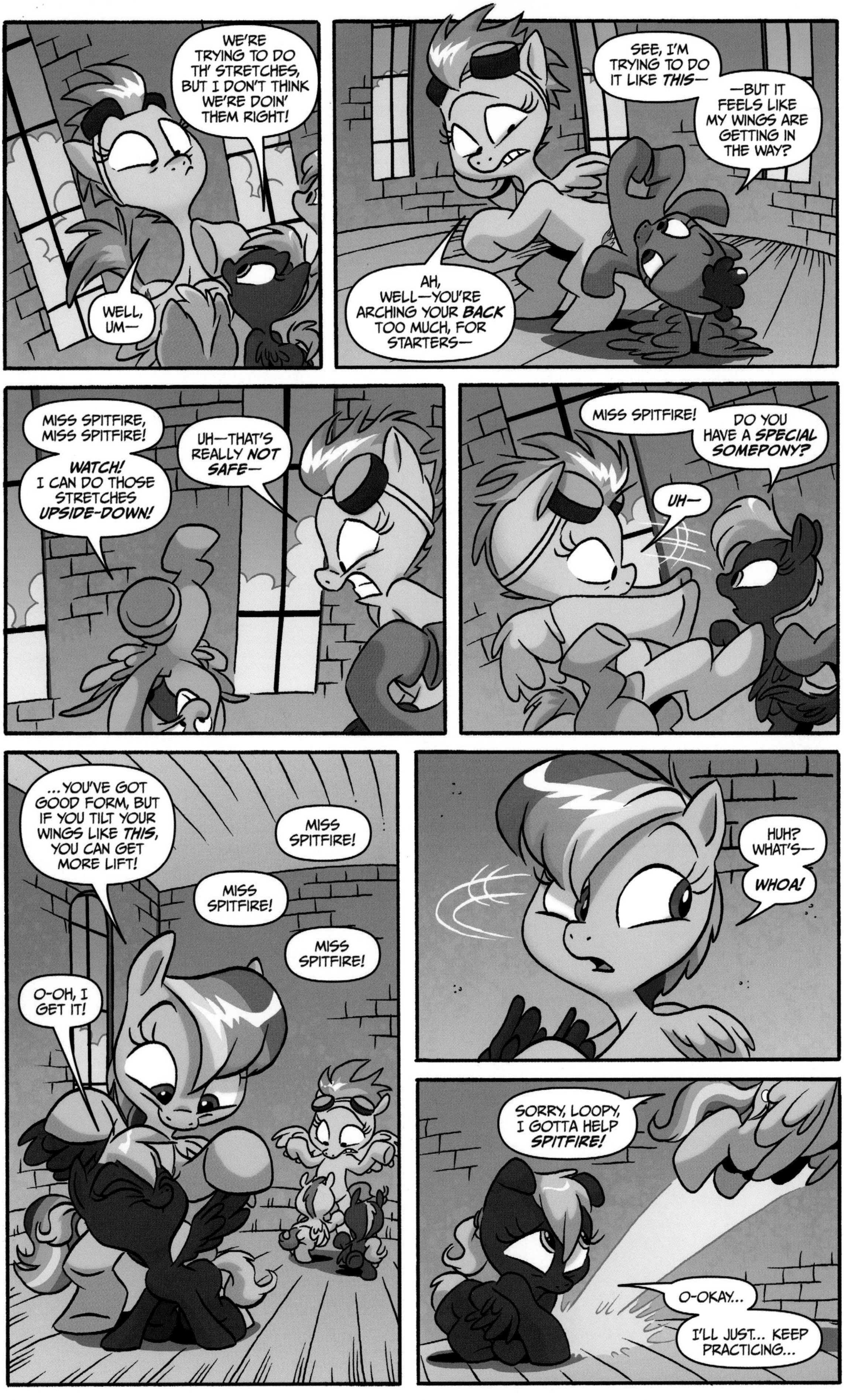
WE'RE TRYING TO DO TH' STRETCHES, BUT I DON'T THINK WE'RE DOIN' THEM RIGHT!
WELL, UM—
SEE, I'M TRYING TO DO IT LIKE *THIS*—
—BUT IT FEELS LIKE MY WINGS ARE GETTING IN THE WAY?
AH, WELL—YOU'RE ARCHING YOUR ***BACK*** TOO MUCH, FOR STARTERS—
MISS SPITFIRE, MISS SPITFIRE!
WATCH! I CAN DO THOSE STRETCHES ***UPSIDE-DOWN!***
UH—THAT'S REALLY ***NOT SAFE***—
MISS SPITFIRE!
DO YOU HAVE A ***SPECIAL SOMEPONY?***
UH—
...YOU'VE GOT GOOD FORM, BUT IF YOU TILT YOUR WINGS LIKE *THIS*, YOU CAN GET MORE LIFT!
MISS SPITFIRE!
MISS SPITFIRE!
MISS SPITFIRE!
O-OH, I GET IT!
HUH? WHAT'S—
WHOA!
SORRY, LOOPY, I GOTTA HELP ***SPITFIRE!***
O-OKAY...
I'LL JUST... KEEP PRACTICING...

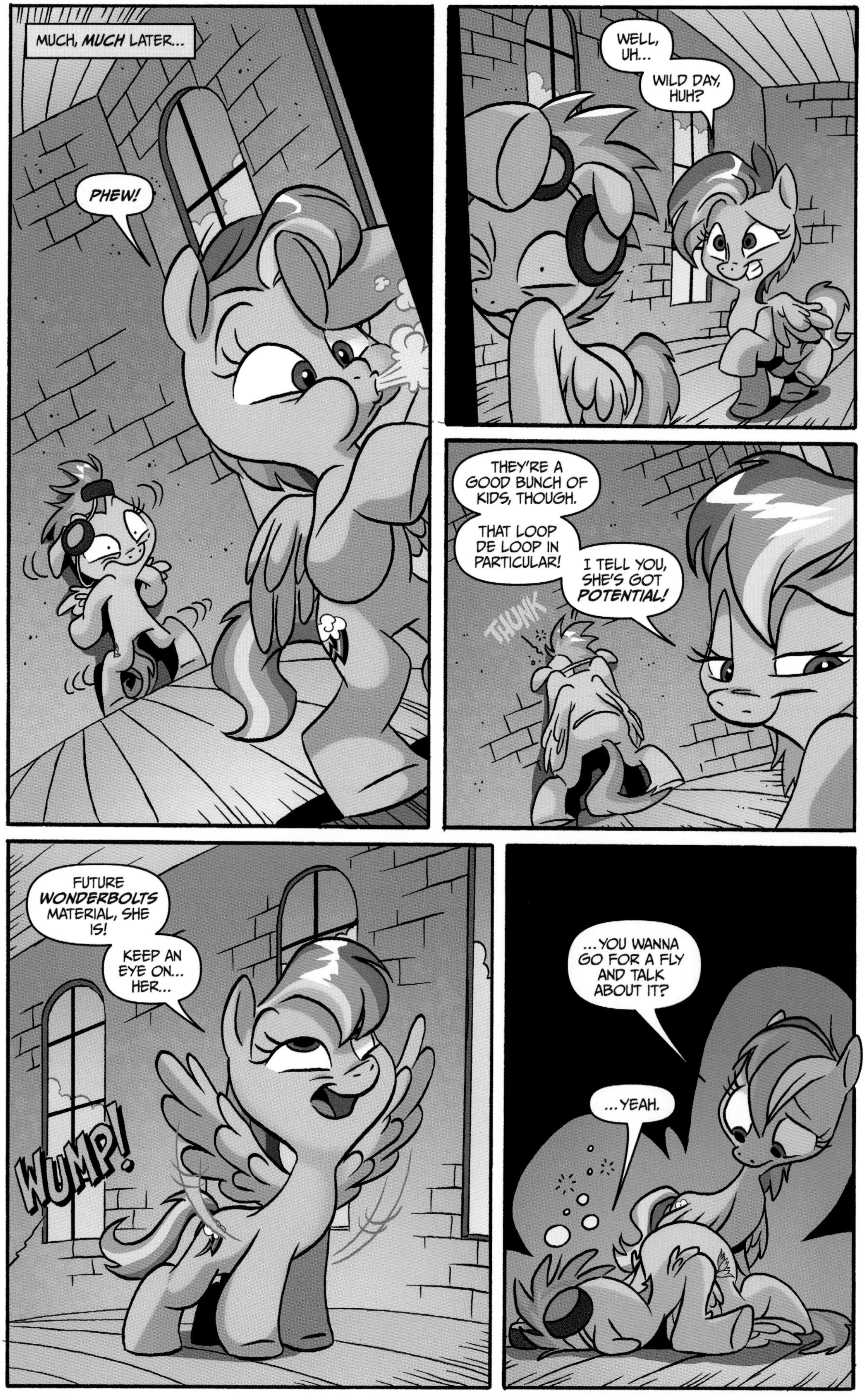
MUCH, *MUCH* LATER...
PHEW!
WELL, UH...
WILD DAY, HUH?
THEY'RE A GOOD BUNCH OF KIDS, THOUGH.
THAT LOOP DE LOOP IN PARTICULAR!
I TELL YOU, SHE'S GOT *POTENTIAL!*
THUNK
FUTURE *WONDERBOLTS* MATERIAL, SHE IS!
KEEP AN EYE ON... HER...
WUMP!
...YOU WANNA GO FOR A FLY AND TALK ABOUT IT?
...YEAH.

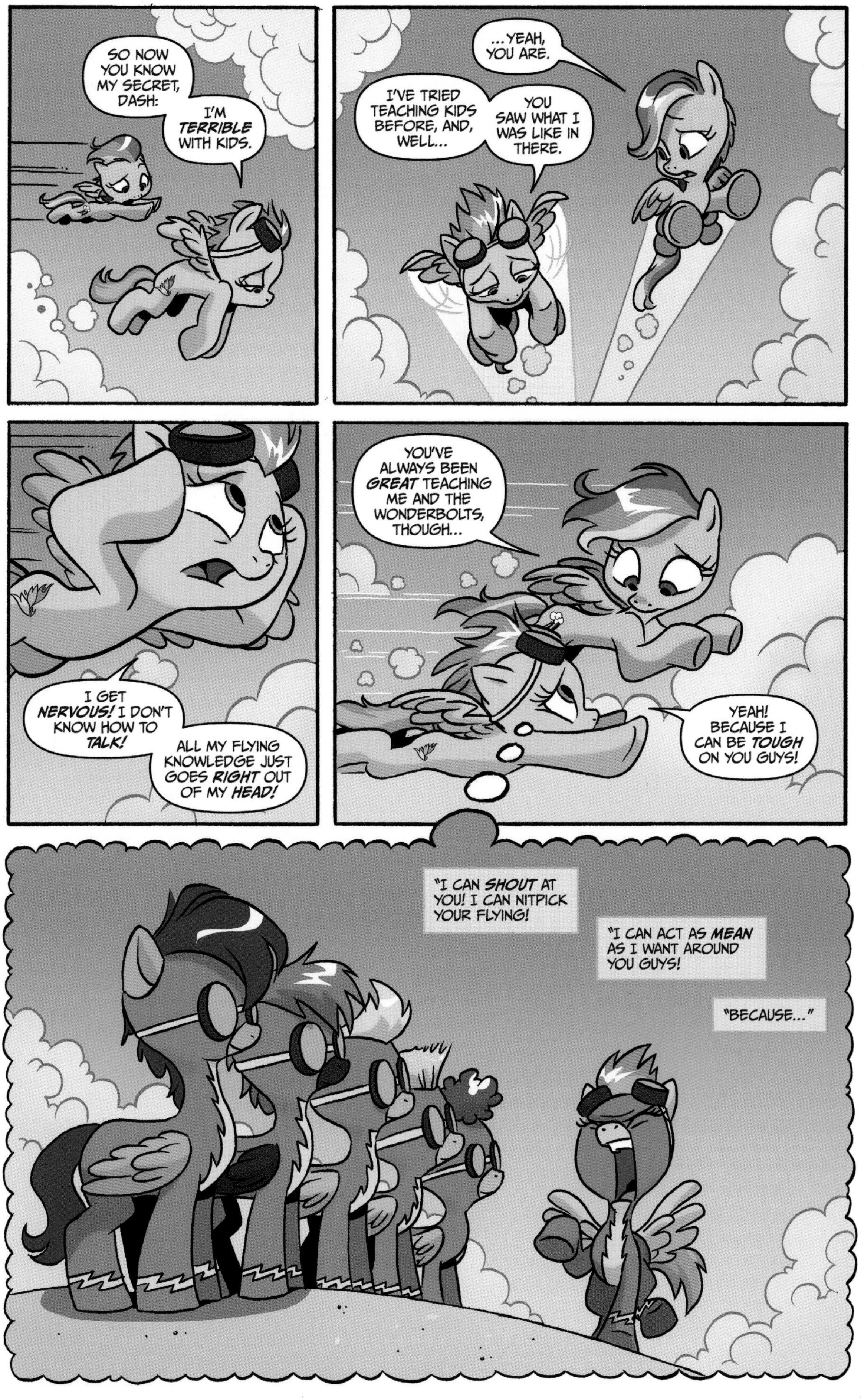
SO NOW YOU KNOW MY SECRET, DASH:
I'M TERRIBLE WITH KIDS.
...YEAH, YOU ARE.
I'VE TRIED TEACHING KIDS BEFORE, AND, WELL...
YOU SAW WHAT I WAS LIKE IN THERE.
I GET NERVOUS! I DON'T KNOW HOW TO TALK!
ALL MY FLYING KNOWLEDGE JUST GOES RIGHT OUT OF MY HEAD!
YOU'VE ALWAYS BEEN GREAT TEACHING ME AND THE WONDERBOLTS, THOUGH...
YEAH! BECAUSE I CAN BE TOUGH ON YOU GUYS!
"I CAN SHOUT AT YOU! I CAN NITPICK YOUR FLYING!
"I CAN ACT AS MEAN AS I WANT AROUND YOU GUYS!
"BECAUSE..."

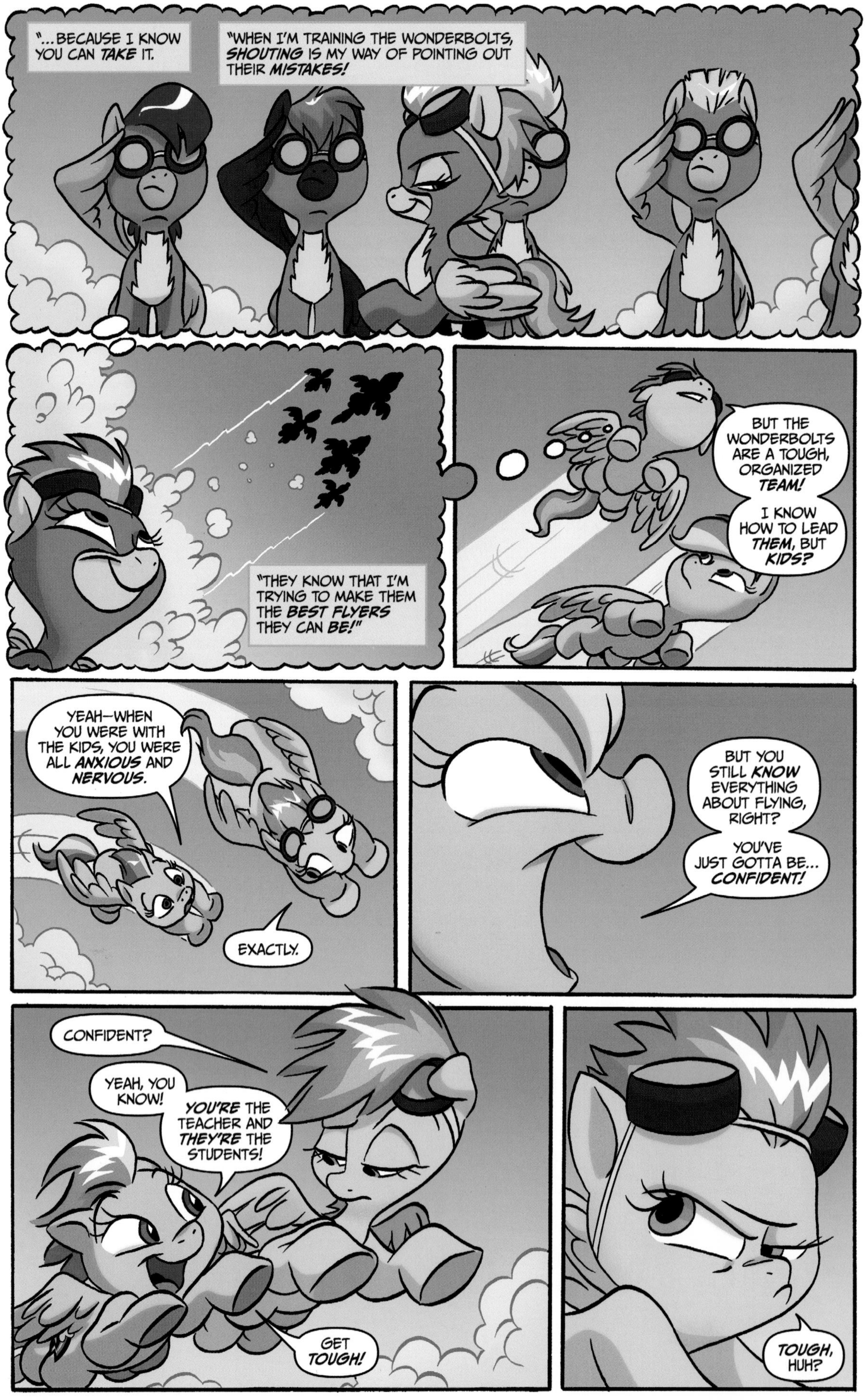

"...BECAUSE I KNOW YOU CAN TAKE IT.
"WHEN I'M TRAINING THE WONDERBOLTS, SHOUTING IS MY WAY OF POINTING OUT THEIR MISTAKES!
"THEY KNOW THAT I'M TRYING TO MAKE THEM THE BEST FLYERS THEY CAN BE!"
BUT THE WONDERBOLTS ARE A TOUGH, ORGANIZED TEAM!
I KNOW HOW TO LEAD THEM, BUT KIDS?
YEAH—WHEN YOU WERE WITH THE KIDS, YOU WERE ALL ANXIOUS AND NERVOUS.
EXACTLY.
BUT YOU STILL KNOW EVERYTHING ABOUT FLYING, RIGHT?
YOU'VE JUST GOTTA BE... CONFIDENT!
CONFIDENT?
YEAH, YOU KNOW!
YOU'RE THE TEACHER AND THEY'RE THE STUDENTS!
GET TOUGH!
TOUGH, HUH?

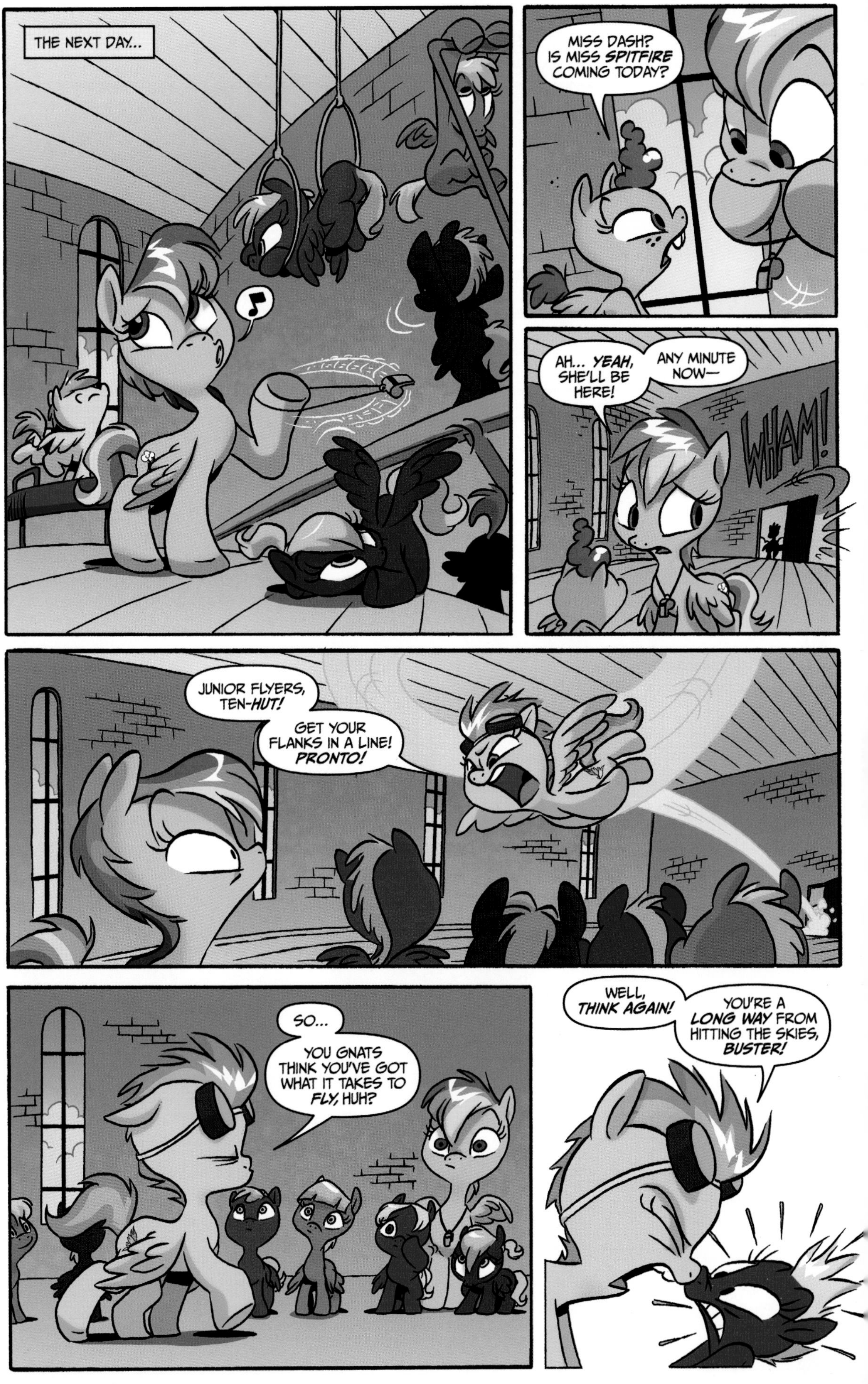
THE NEXT DAY...
MISS DASH? IS MISS SPITFIRE COMING TODAY?
AH... YEAH, SHE'LL BE HERE!
ANY MINUTE NOW—
WHAM!
JUNIOR FLYERS, TEN-HUT!
GET YOUR FLANKS IN A LINE! PRONTO!
SO...
YOU GNATS THINK YOU'VE GOT WHAT IT TAKES TO FLY, HUH?
WELL, THINK AGAIN!
YOU'RE A LONG WAY FROM HITTING THE SKIES, BUSTER!

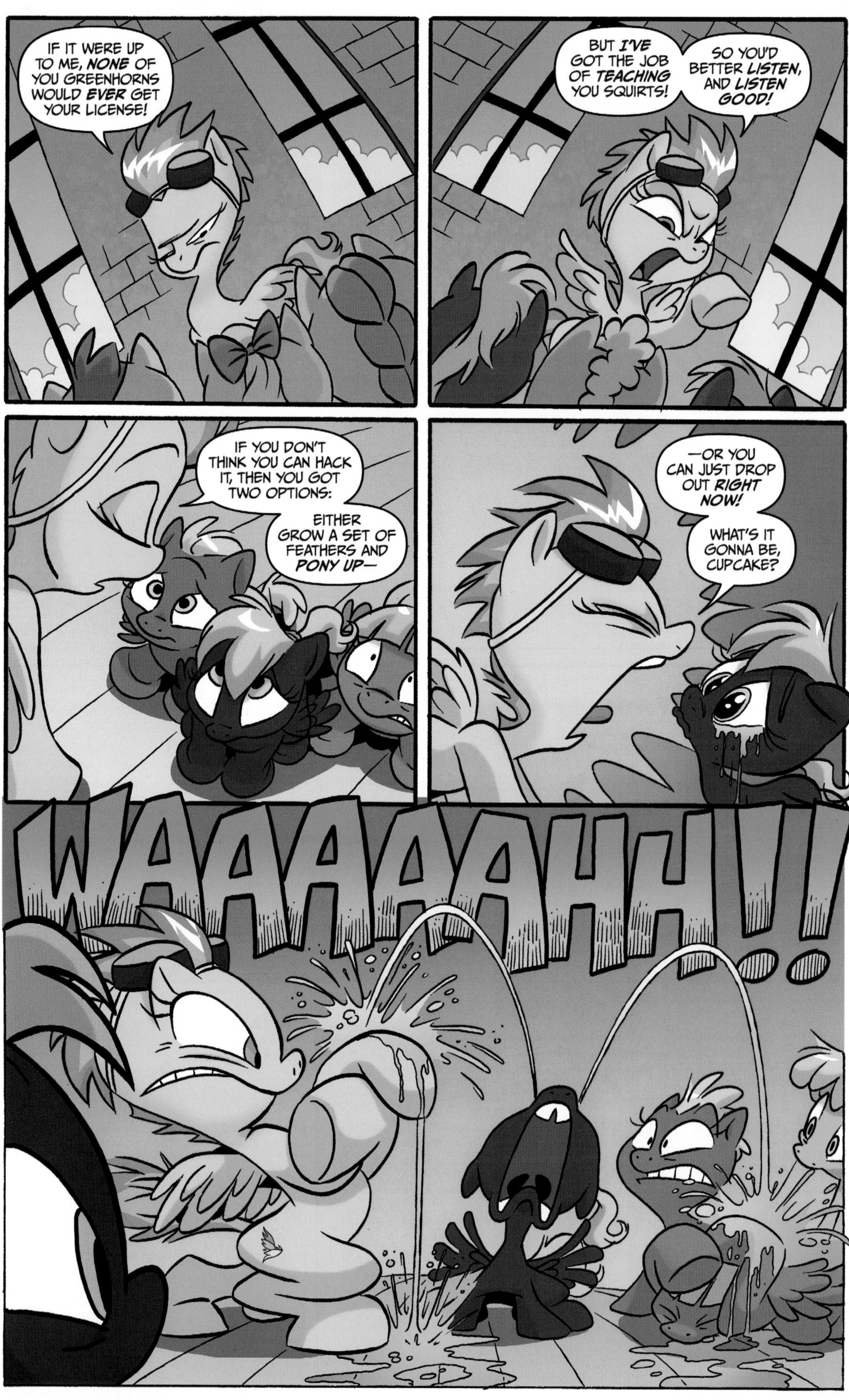
IF IT WERE UP TO ME, NONE OF YOU GREENHORNS WOULD EVER GET YOUR LICENSE!
BUT I'VE GOT THE JOB OF TEACHING YOU SQUIRTS!
SO YOU'D BETTER LISTEN, AND LISTEN GOOD!
IF YOU DON'T THINK YOU CAN HACK IT, THEN YOU GOT TWO OPTIONS:
EITHER GROW A SET OF FEATHERS AND PONY UP—
—OR YOU CAN JUST DROP OUT RIGHT NOW!
WHAT'S IT GONNA BE, CUPCAKE?
WAAAAAHH!!

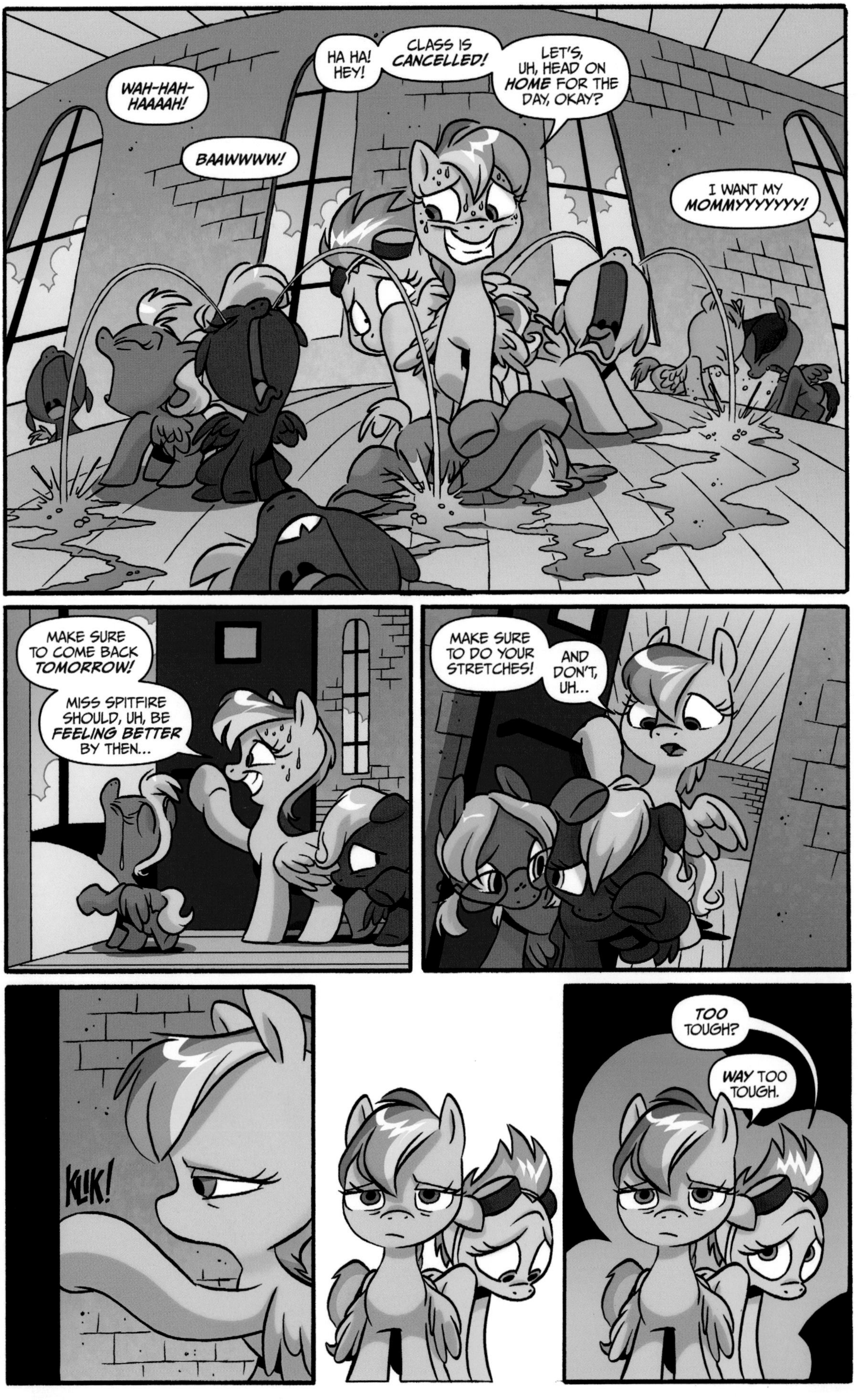
WAH-HAH-HAAAAH!
BAAWWWW!
HA HA! HEY!
CLASS IS CANCELLED!
LET'S, UH, HEAD ON HOME FOR THE DAY, OKAY?
I WANT MY MOMMYYYYYYY!
MAKE SURE TO COME BACK TOMORROW!
MISS SPITFIRE SHOULD, UH, BE FEELING BETTER BY THEN...
MAKE SURE TO DO YOUR STRETCHES!
AND DON'T, UH...
KLIK!
TOO TOUGH?
WAY TOO TOUGH.

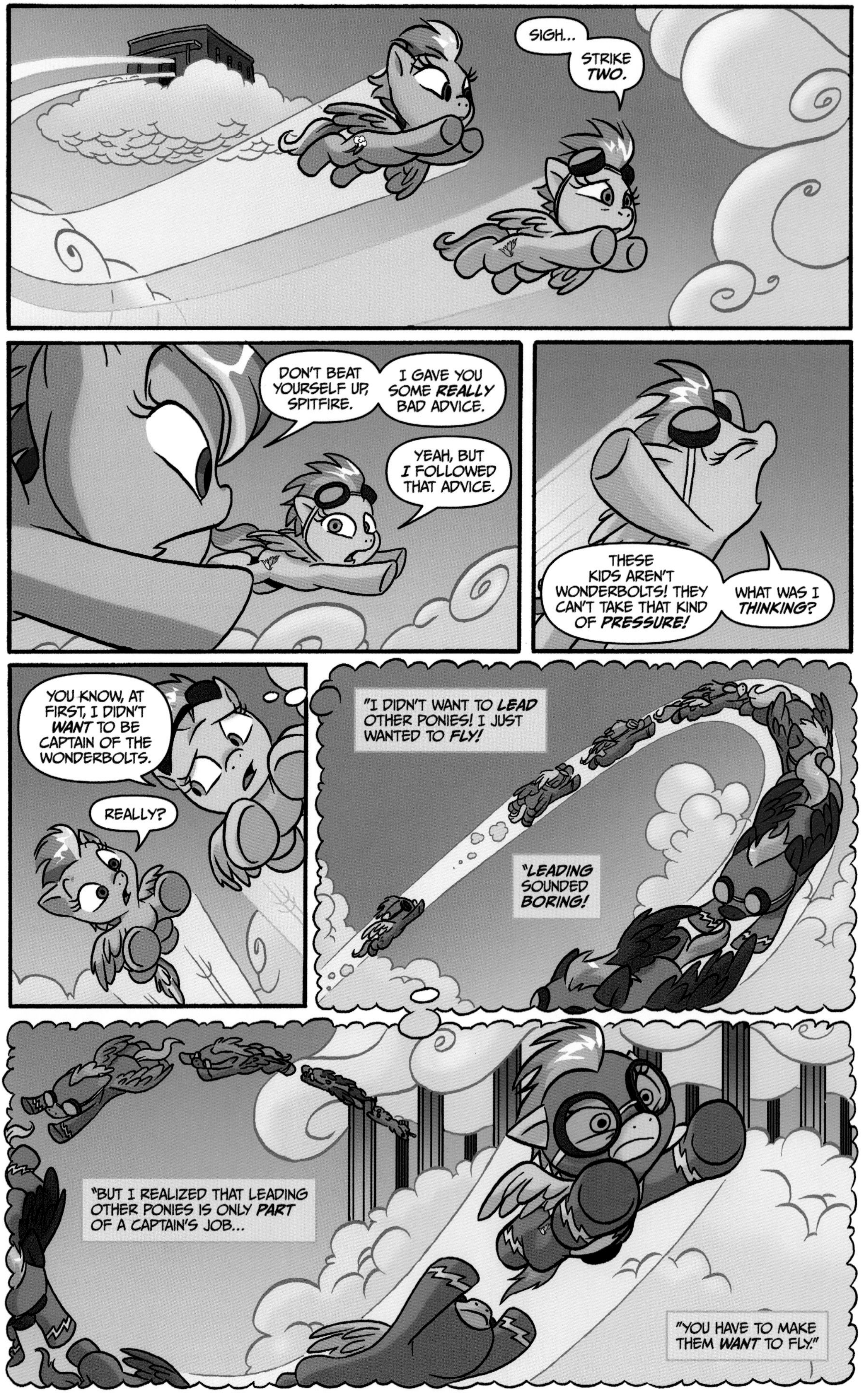
SIGH...
STRIKE TWO.
DON'T BEAT YOURSELF UP, SPITFIRE.
I GAVE YOU SOME REALLY BAD ADVICE.
YEAH, BUT I FOLLOWED THAT ADVICE.
THESE KIDS AREN'T WONDERBOLTS! THEY CAN'T TAKE THAT KIND OF PRESSURE!
WHAT WAS I THINKING?
YOU KNOW, AT FIRST, I DIDN'T WANT TO BE CAPTAIN OF THE WONDERBOLTS.
REALLY?
"I DIDN'T WANT TO LEAD OTHER PONIES! I JUST WANTED TO FLY!
"LEADING SOUNDED BORING!
"BUT I REALIZED THAT LEADING OTHER PONIES IS ONLY PART OF A CAPTAIN'S JOB...
"YOU HAVE TO MAKE THEM WANT TO FLY."

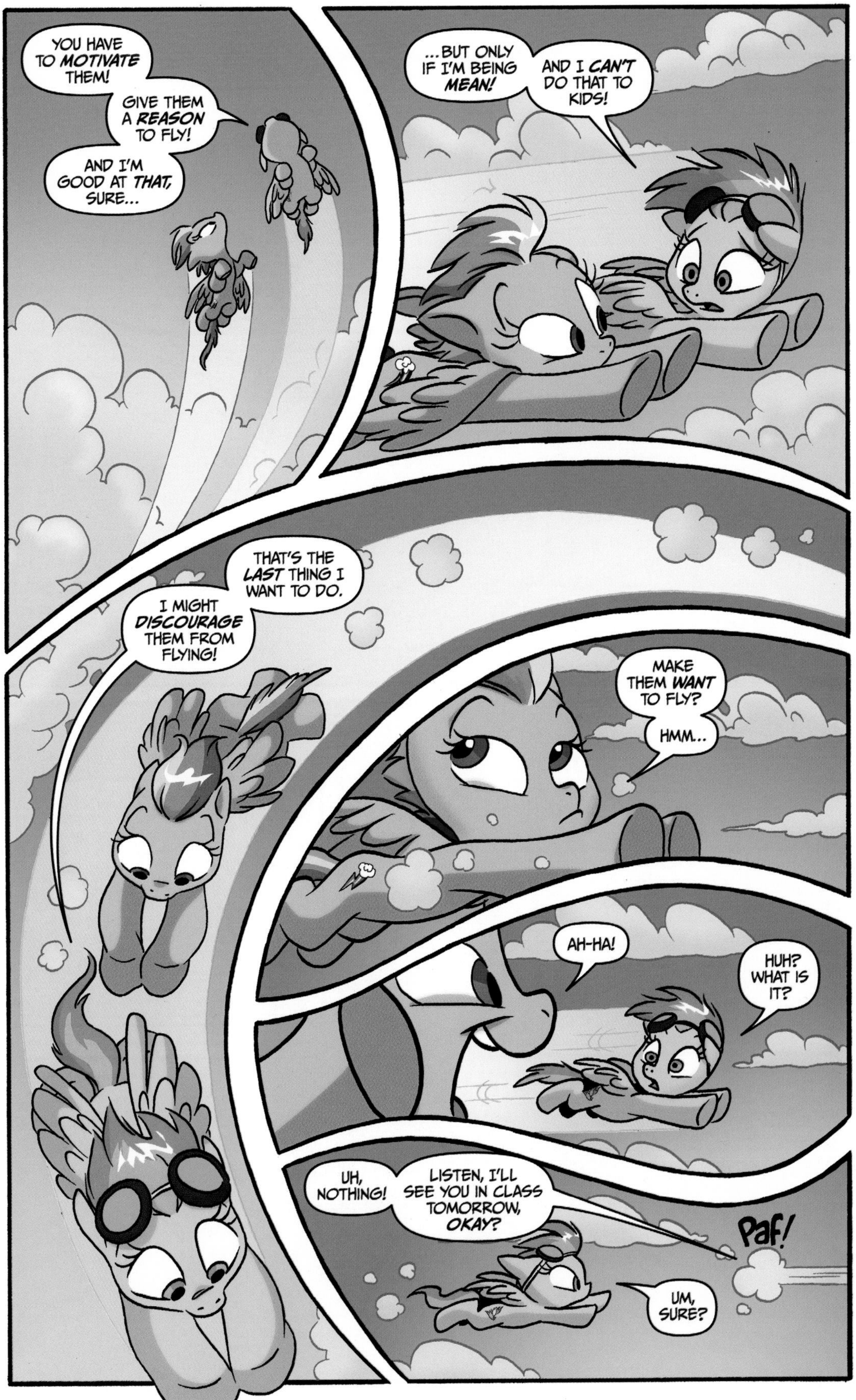
YOU HAVE TO MOTIVATE THEM!
GIVE THEM A REASON TO FLY!
AND I'M GOOD AT THAT, SURE...
...BUT ONLY IF I'M BEING MEAN!
AND I CAN'T DO THAT TO KIDS!
THAT'S THE LAST THING I WANT TO DO.
I MIGHT DISCOURAGE THEM FROM FLYING!
MAKE THEM WANT TO FLY?
HMM...
AH-HA!
HUH? WHAT IS IT?
UH, NOTHING!
LISTEN, I'LL SEE YOU IN CLASS TOMORROW, OKAY?
PAF!
UM, SURE?

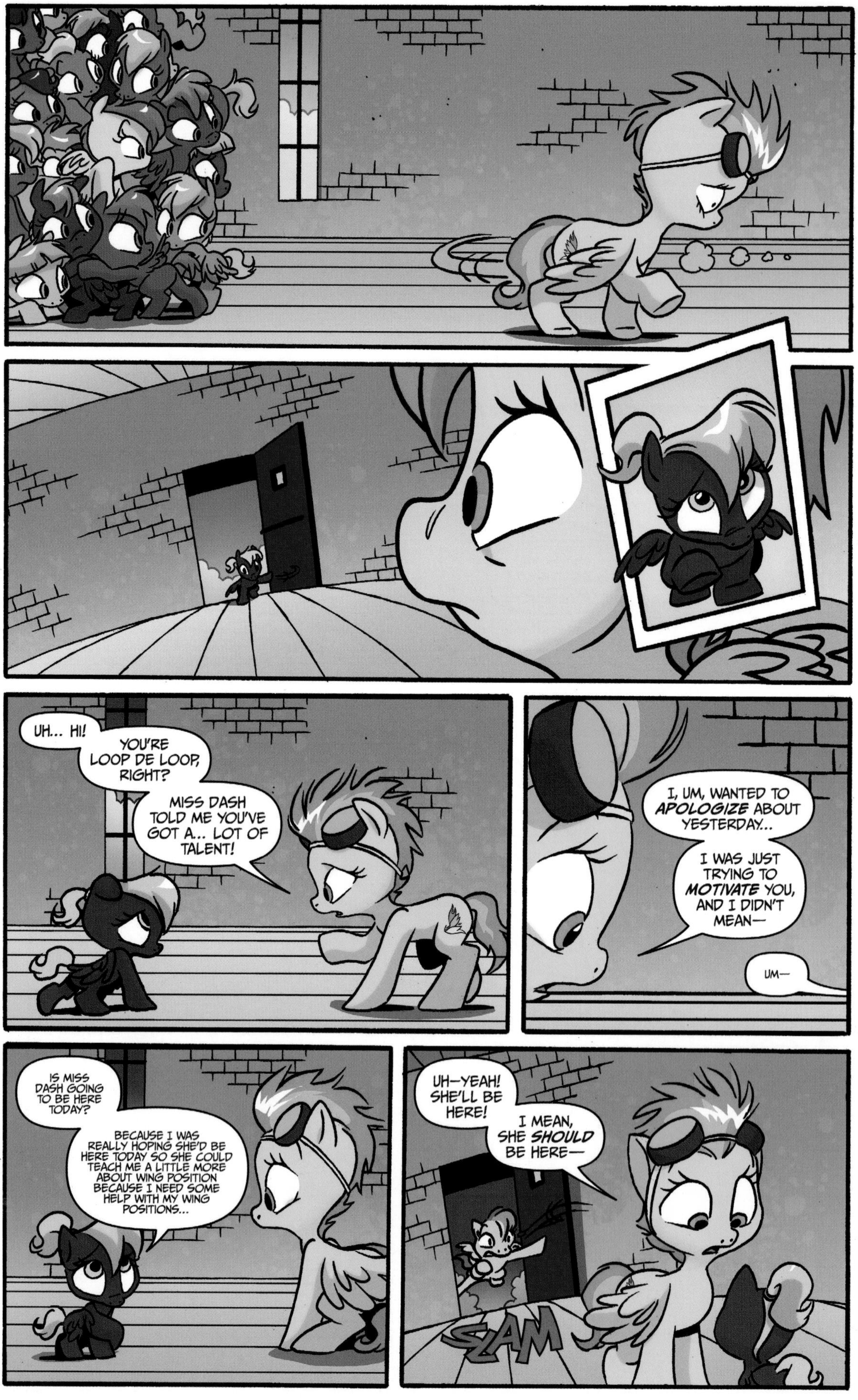
UH... HI!
YOU'RE LOOP DE LOOP, RIGHT?
MISS DASH TOLD ME YOU'VE GOT A... LOT OF TALENT!
I, UM, WANTED TO *APOLOGIZE* ABOUT YESTERDAY...
I WAS JUST TRYING TO *MOTIVATE* YOU, AND I DIDN'T MEAN—
UM—
IS MISS DASH GOING TO BE HERE TODAY?
BECAUSE I WAS REALLY HOPING SHE'D BE HERE TODAY SO SHE COULD TEACH ME A LITTLE MORE ABOUT WING POSITION BECAUSE I NEED SOME HELP WITH MY WING POSITIONS...
UH—YEAH! SHE'LL BE HERE!
I MEAN, SHE *SHOULD* BE HERE—
SLAM

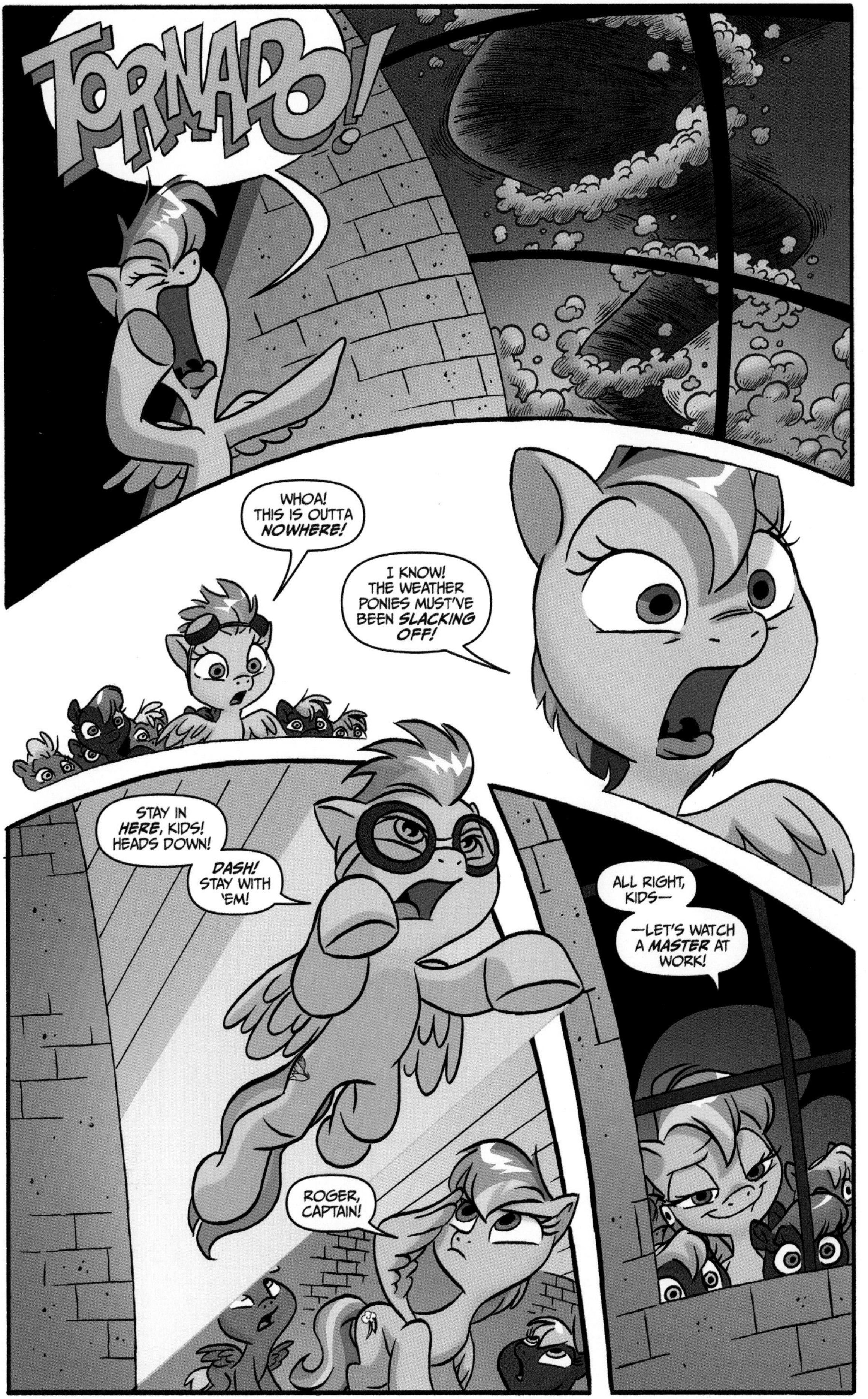
TORNADO!
WHOA! THIS IS OUTTA NOWHERE!
I KNOW! THE WEATHER PONIES MUST'VE BEEN SLACKING OFF!
STAY IN HERE, KIDS! HEADS DOWN!
DASH! STAY WITH 'EM!
ROGER, CAPTAIN!
ALL RIGHT, KIDS—
—LET'S WATCH A MASTER AT WORK!

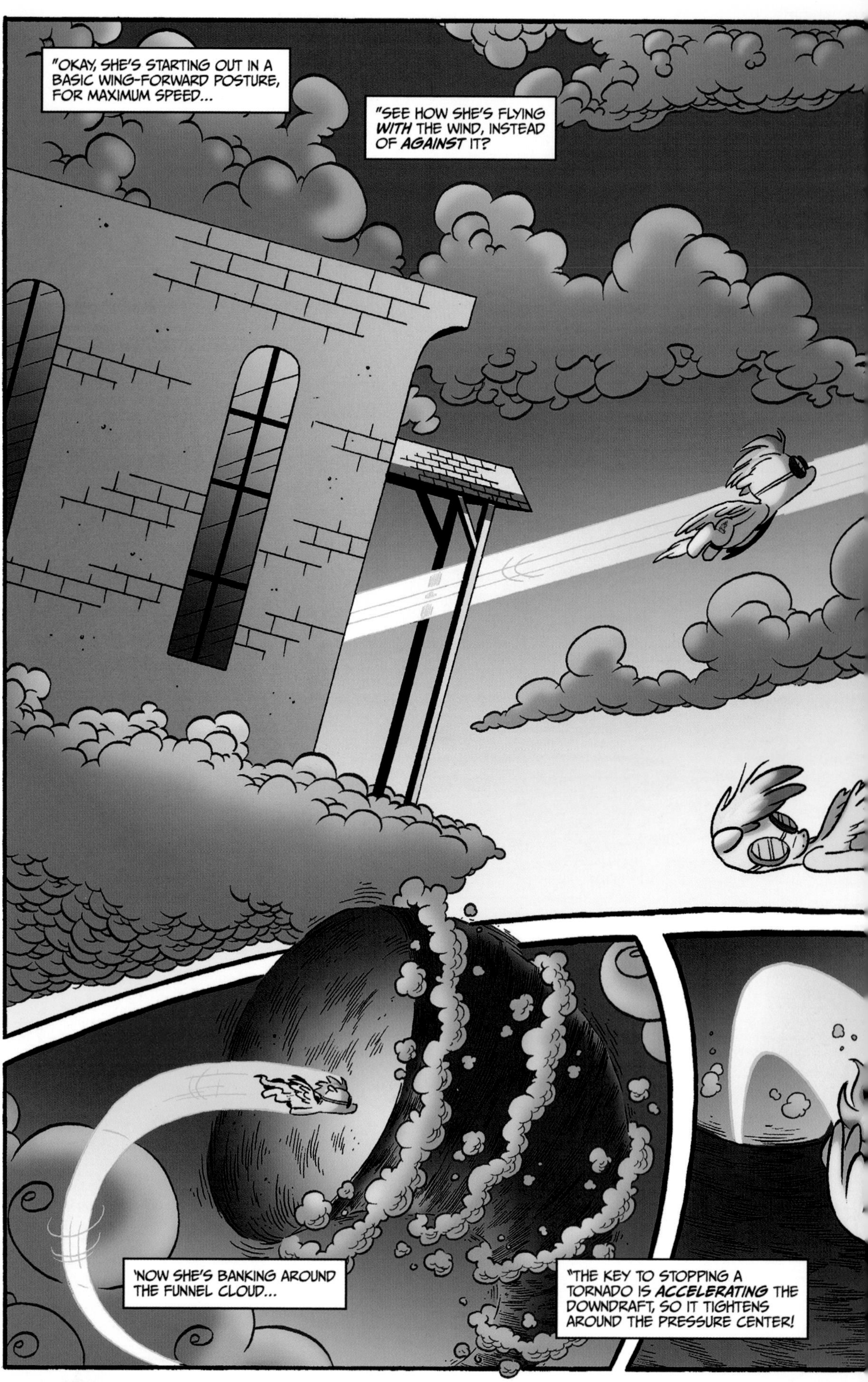
"OKAY, SHE'S STARTING OUT IN A BASIC WING-FORWARD POSTURE, FOR MAXIMUM SPEED...
"SEE HOW SHE'S FLYING **WITH** THE WIND, INSTEAD OF **AGAINST** IT?
'NOW SHE'S BANKING AROUND THE FUNNEL CLOUD...
"THE KEY TO STOPPING A TORNADO IS **ACCELERATING** THE DOWNDRAFT, SO IT TIGHTENS AROUND THE PRESSURE CENTER!

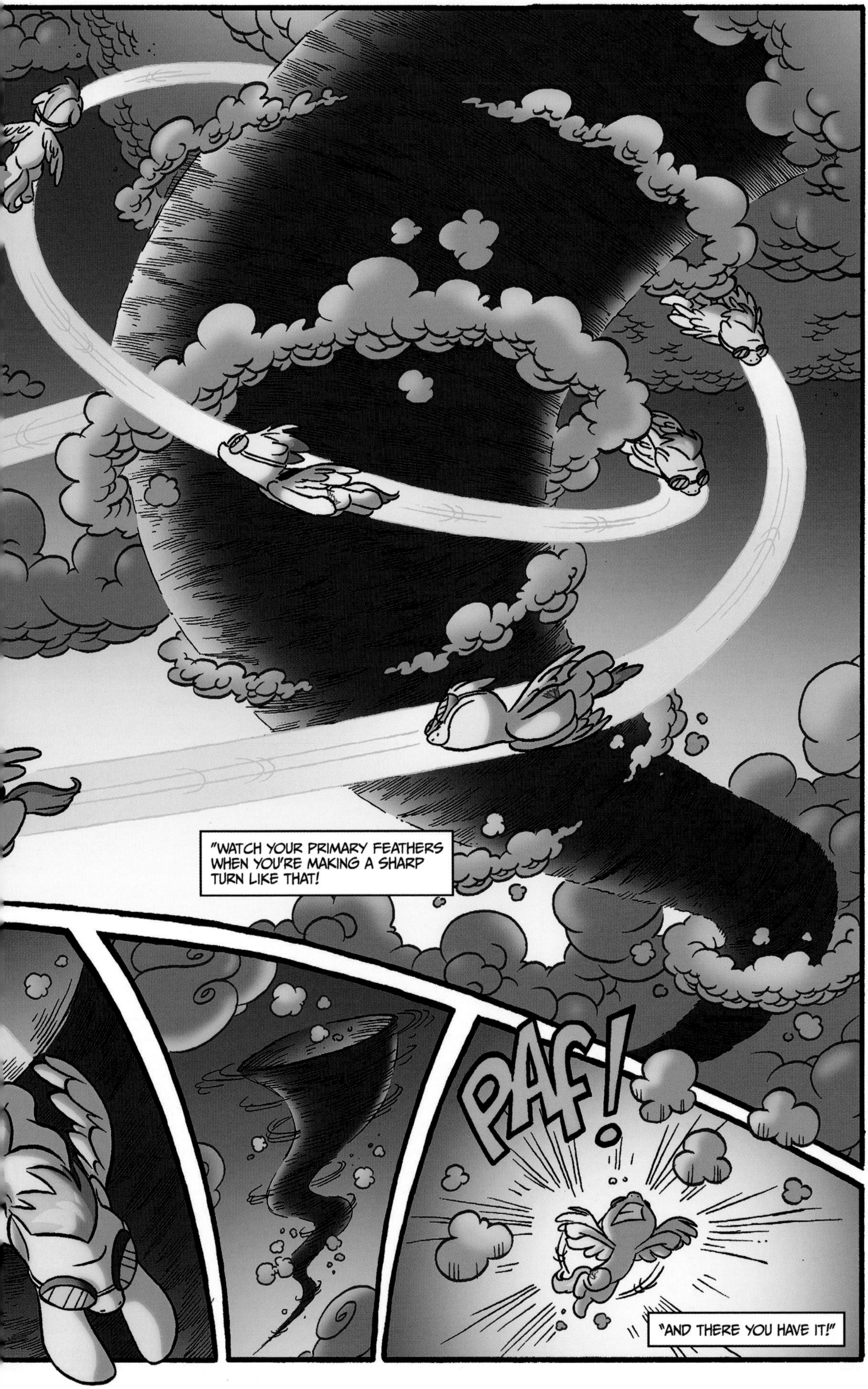
"WATCH YOUR PRIMARY FEATHERS
WHEN YOU'RE MAKING A SHARP
TURN LIKE THAT!
PAF!
"AND THERE YOU HAVE IT!"

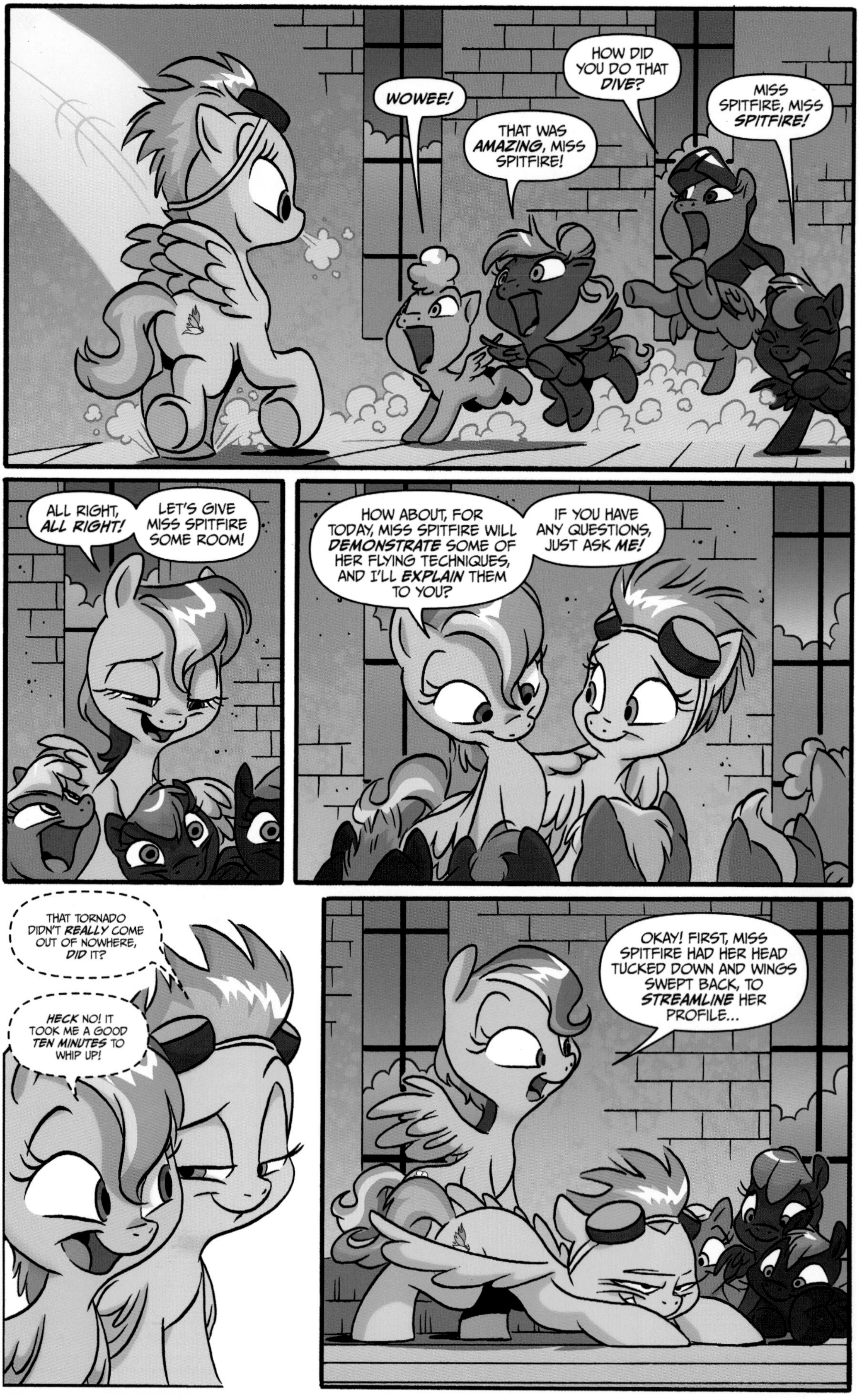
WOWEE!
THAT WAS AMAZING, MISS SPITFIRE!
HOW DID YOU DO THAT DIVE?
MISS SPITFIRE, MISS SPITFIRE!
ALL RIGHT, ALL RIGHT!
LET'S GIVE MISS SPITFIRE SOME ROOM!
HOW ABOUT, FOR TODAY, MISS SPITFIRE WILL DEMONSTRATE SOME OF HER FLYING TECHNIQUES, AND I'LL EXPLAIN THEM TO YOU?
IF YOU HAVE ANY QUESTIONS, JUST ASK ME!
THAT TORNADO DIDN'T REALLY COME OUT OF NOWHERE, DID IT?
HECK NO! IT TOOK ME A GOOD TEN MINUTES TO WHIP UP!
OKAY! FIRST, MISS SPITFIRE HAD HER HEAD TUCKED DOWN AND WINGS SWEPT BACK, TO STREAMLINE HER PROFILE...

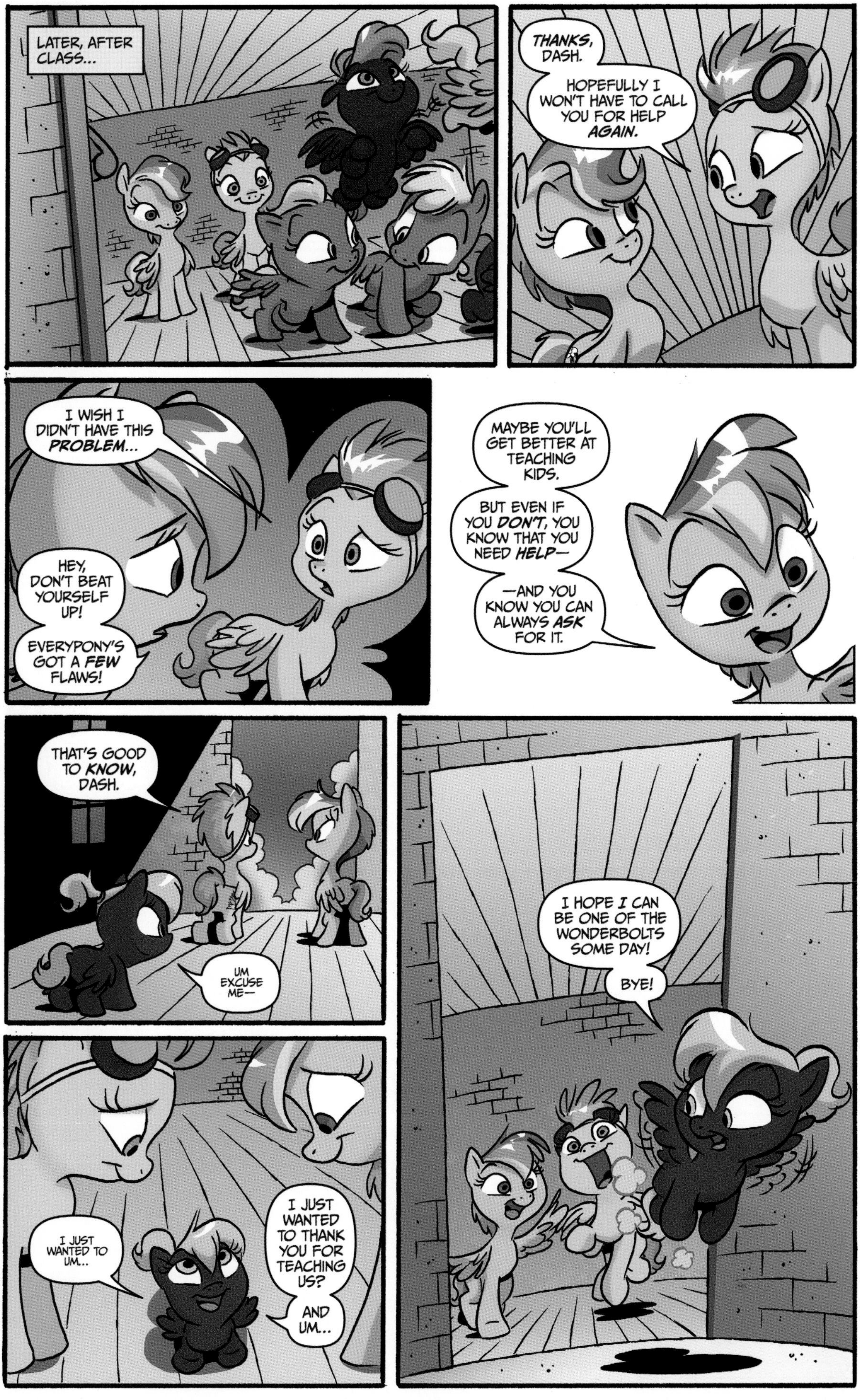
LATER, AFTER CLASS...
THANKS, DASH.
HOPEFULLY I WON'T HAVE TO CALL YOU FOR HELP AGAIN.
I WISH I DIDN'T HAVE THIS PROBLEM...
HEY, DON'T BEAT YOURSELF UP!
EVERYPONY'S GOT A FEW FLAWS!
MAYBE YOU'LL GET BETTER AT TEACHING KIDS.
BUT EVEN IF YOU DON'T, YOU KNOW THAT YOU NEED HELP—
—AND YOU KNOW YOU CAN ALWAYS ASK FOR IT.
THAT'S GOOD TO KNOW, DASH.
UM EXCUSE ME—
I JUST WANTED TO UM...
I JUST WANTED TO THANK YOU FOR TEACHING US?
AND UM...
I HOPE I CAN BE ONE OF THE WONDERBOLTS SOME DAY!
BYE!

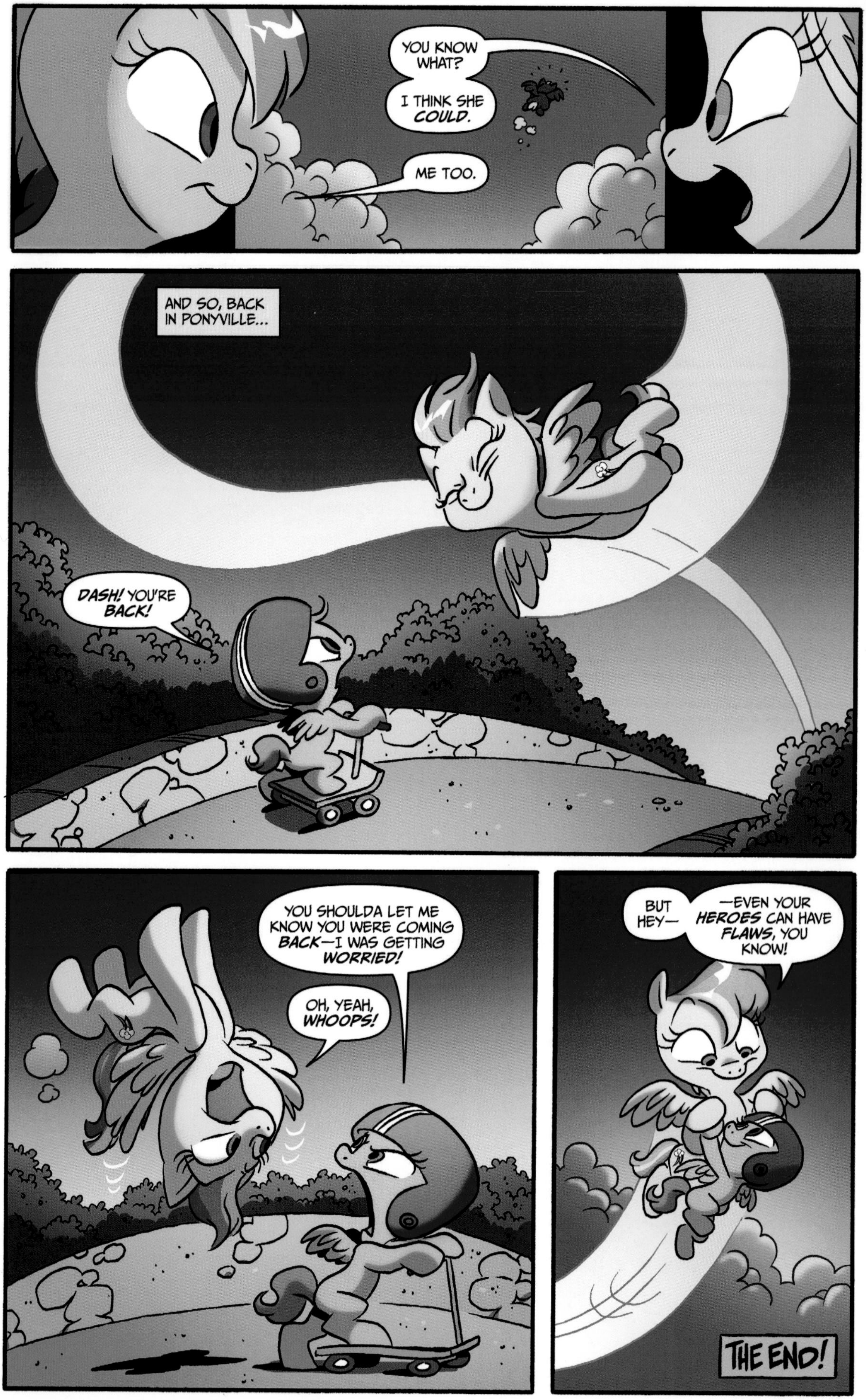
YOU KNOW WHAT?
I THINK SHE COULD.
ME TOO.
AND SO, BACK IN PONYVILLE...
DASH! YOU'RE BACK!
YOU SHOULDA LET ME KNOW YOU WERE COMING BACK—I WAS GETTING WORRIED!
OH, YEAH, WHOOPS!
BUT HEY—
—EVEN YOUR HEROES CAN HAVE FLAWS, YOU KNOW!
THE END!